The Bush

"That is a good camp," said Raj.
"We should get wood for the
camp fire."

The kids got the wood and put it on the camp fire. "We should get water from the brook," said Raj.

"What shall we cook?" asked Raj.
"We could have pasta and tuna
fish." Chen put a pot on the fire.

Chen cooked the pasta and put
the tuna on top. Yum! Just then,
there was a crackle in the bush.

The kids took one good look at
the bush. What could it be?
They ran into the tent.

It was not a bull! It was not a
wolf! A little mouse ran from
the bush. Pasta! Yum!

Questions for discussion:

- Why do the kids need wood?

- Why do the kids go to the brook?

- What do you think Raj and Chen feel when they see a mouse?

Game with /oo/ words

Play as 'Concentration' or use for reading practice. Enlarge and photocopy the page twice on two different colors of card.
Cut the cards up to play.
Ensure the players sound out the words.

book	put	could
would	cook	bull
full	should	brook
wood	push	couldn't

Before reading this book, the reader needs to know:

- sounds can be spelled by more than one letter.
- the spellings <oo>, <oul> and <u> can represent the sound /oo/ (look).

This book introduces:

- the spellings <oo>, <oul> and <u> for the sound /oo/ (look).
- text at 2-syllable level.

Words the reader may need help with:

said, for, fire, water, what, tuna, there, was crackle, one, be, into, wolf, little, mouse

Vocabulary:

brook   – a small stream
crackle – a cracking sound like a twig breaking
bull   – a male cow, ox or elephant

Talk about the story:

When Raj and Chen go camping, something scares them.
What could it be?

Reading Practice

Practice blending these sounds into words:

oo	oul	u
took	could	full
wood	should	put
cook	would	bull
good	couldn't	bush
shook	wouldn't	pull
stood	shouldn't	push
brook		helpful